BY CORI BROOKE

art by Katie Alexander

THIS GIRL CAN!

FIVE MILE

This girl cares for sick dogs and sick cats,

This girl wears big boots and hard hats,

This girl discovers new planets and stars,

This girl drives fast in red racing cars.

This girl practises and enforces the law,

This girl says 'stick your tongue out and say AAWWWW',

This girl kicks winning soccer goals,

This girl digs enormous wide holes.

This girl flies shiny new planes,

This girl controls tall swinging cranes,

Each of these girls is
bold and smart,

They believed in
themselves and followed
their hearts.

This girl is the lead singer of her own rock band.

This girl grows veggies and fruit out on the land.

This girl directs movies for the big screen,

This girl invented a life-saving vaccine,

This girl is a video-game designer,

This girl is a precious metal miner.

This girl loves numbers – her passion is Pi,

3.1415
4338327950
37516

This girl keeps planes safe in the clear blue sky,

This girl paints
beautiful pictures
and draws,

This girl
argues for
new Federal
laws.

Each of these girls is bold and smart.
They believed in themselves
And followed their hearts.

Look in the mirror
Ask: 'What can this girl be?'

You can be anything,
Your future is free.

There is no limit
to what you can
achieve,

If you work hard,
and truly believe.

The key is to believe
That dreams can come true.

Because you are also bold and smart,
Believe in yourself
And follow your heart.

FIVE
MILE

Five Mile, the publishing division of Regency Media

www.fivemile.com.au

First published 2020

Written by Cori Brooke
Illustrations by Katie Alexander
Text copyright © Cori Brooke, 2020
Illustration copyright ©Katie Alexander, 2020

ISBN: 978-1-92238-525-3 (hbk)

Printed in China 5 4 3

NATIONAL
LIBRARY
OF AUSTRALIA

A catalogue record for this book is available from the National Library of Australia